Henry J. Wehman

Brudder Bone' s

4-11-44 Joker

Henry J. Wehman

Brudder Bone' s
4-11-44 Joker

ISBN/EAN: 9783744746007

Printed in Europe, USA, Canada, Australia, Japan

Cover: Foto ©Andreas Hilbeck / pixelio.de

More available books at **www.hansebooks.com**

WEHMAN'S

Brudder Bones'

"4-11-44"

JOKER

CONTAINING A JOLLY LOT OF

Sable Conundrums, Ethiopian Jokes, Burnt
Cork Comicalities and Darkey Dialogues.

———

Published by

HENRY J. WEHMAN,
NEW YORK.

Popular Books.—Sent post-paid at the Prices Marked

Wehman's Book on Dogs. How to keep and train them. Descriptions of the various breeds, their characteristics and points, and their management in health and disease. Sent by mail, post-paid, on receipt of 10 Cents.

Wehman's Book on Rabbits. How to breed and manage them. Tells how to arrange their houses, and gives careful instructions as to their food and treatment, both in health and disease. Sent by mail, post-paid, on receipt of 10 Cents.

Wehman's Book on Pigeons. For pleasure and profit. Tells of the different varieties, both wild and domestic, with full directions for their breeding and care. Sent by mail, post-paid, on receipt of 10 Cents. U. S. postage stamps taken same as cash.

Wehman's Book on Song Birds. Tells how to rear and treat all the birds that are capable of being domesticated as household songters, in health and disease. Sent by mail, post-paid, on receipt of 10 Cents. U. S. postage stamps taken same as cash.

Wehman's Book on Pets. Their care and management, including squirrels, guinea pigs, white mice, etc. Also, instructions for aquariums, and the care of silk worms. Sent by mail, post-paid, on receipt of **10 Cents.** U. S. postage stamps taken same as cash.

De Witt's Complete American Farrier and Horse DOCTOR. An American book for American horsemen; with copious notes from the best English and American authorities, showing plainly how to breed, rear, buy, sell, cure, shoe, and keep that most useful and valuable animal, the horse. With many superior illustrations. Sent by mail, post-paid, on receipt of **25 Cents.**

Wehman's Practical Poultry Book. Many old-fashioned farmers are inclined to discredit the statement that there is money in poultry. Why? Because they are not up to the new and improved ideas in poultry management. A little trial of the rules laid down in this book will soon dispel all misgivings in this direction, and tend to convince the most skeptical that there is money in poultry-keeping. Sent by mail, post-paid, on receipt of **25 Cents.**

Wehman's American Live Stock Manual. Many a man has lost a valuable animal for no other reason than he did not know how to take care of it when well, or treat it properly when sick. The cost of this book is but a trifle, but it is simply worth its weight in gold to any man who owns cattle of any kind, for it is a complete text-book, containing the fullest information regarding the rearing of live stock, both in health and disease. Sent by mail, post-paid, on receipt of **25 Cts.**

Wehman's Complete Dancing Master and Call BOOK. All the figures of the German and every new and fashionable dance known in Europe or America. This book is written in so simple a manner that any child, by reading it, can become an expert in dancing without the aid of a teacher. All the latest and fashionable dances are minutely described by illustration from life, explaining positions in round dances, etc., and this original method enables persons to learn the waltz by practicing it a very few times. Hints on the management of balls, etc. Sent by mail, post-paid, on receipt of **25 Cents.**

ADDRESS ALL ORDERS TO

HENRY J. WEHMAN, Publisher, 108 Park Row, New York

BRUDDER BONE'S
"4-11-44" JOKER.

Spell L-a-d-y.

"I understand, sir, that you have been to college?"

"Oh yes, sir—l've been all frough scollege."

"Then I suppose that you can spell pretty well?"

"I can spell anyting dat you can ax me."

"Well, spell Lady, that's an easy word."

"We didn't hab any ob dem in de school I went to."

"L-a-d-y—that spells Lady."

"Ob course it does; any body ought to know dat."

"What does A-p-p-l-e—P-i-e spell?"

"Lady, to be sure."

"No, it spells *Apple Pie*. What does Pumpkin Pie spell?"

"Punkin Pie."

"Peach Pie?"

"Peach Pie."

"Mince Pie?"

"Mincen Pie."

"Now then, what does L-a-d-y spell?"

"Custard Pie."

Mistaken Identity.

"In 1864," says a correspondent of WILD OATS, "I was in the ——Hospital, near Richmond, Va., and, being convalescent, I was seated one day in front of my quarters when I observed a North Carolinian come out of his quarters, opposite, and take a look about the premises. Finally he spied a sick Virginian (yellow as saffron from having the jaundice), seated a short distance away. Thinking, evidently, that he had met a companion from the Palmetto State, the North Carolinian, with that peculiar nasal twang which beats the down East Yankee for its intensity, approached him :

"I say, mister, don't yew belong tew the 42d North Carolina Regiment ?"

The Virginian was mad as a hornet, and, looking the daggers he could not gesticulate, he said :

"No, you accursed fool ! I've been sick is what makes me *look so !*"

Palmetto drew off his inquiries, satisfied.

A Quaker Clincher.—A skeptical young collegian confronted an old Quaker with the statement that he did not believe in the Bible.

The Quaker said :

" Does thee believe in France ?"

" Yes, for though I have not seen it, I have seen others that have ; besides there is plenty of corroborative proof that such a country does exist."

" Then thee will not believe anything thee and others have not seen ?"

" No, to be sure I won't."

" Did thee ever see thy own brains ?"

" No."

" Ever see anybody that did ?"

" No."

" Does thee believe thee has any."

The young man left.

If you spend an evening out, never finish it with a reel.

Patriotic.

" Massa, I was to a party de oder night."

" Did you have a rich time ?"

" Didn't do nofin else."

" I suppose you had a supper there ?"

" Yes, sir, and such a supper, and wine flew like water."

" Was there any sentiment given at the table ?"

"Guess not; I didn't see dat dish on de bill ob fair."

" You don't understand—I mean toasts."

" Oh, I know now what you mean. When day was drinkin' somebody would say, ' Here's to us,' etc."

" Yes, exactly. I suppose you had your turn ?"

" Yes, sir."

" What was the toast given by you ?"

" It was dis—

De ships ob our navy,
De ladies ob our land ;
May de former be full rigg'd,
And de latter be well mann'd."

Our office boy's brother is a boy in a store further up town. We overheard them comparing notes of matters and things the other day, and says our boy's brother, " Well, I know that it is rather rough on a fellow to be bossed around by everybody in the store, but, by jingo, don't I get even when the ash-man comes in the morning, eh ? You just bet !"

Chicago theatre audiences are judged from a moral point of view by the number of those that go out " to see a man." On a recent occasion, at the principal theatre, the whole audience, except two men, went out to drink. On investigation, it was found that, of these two, one was already drunk, and the other had an unsettled account at the bar and dare not go.

A young lady from the country now visiting the city writes home thusly : " Nobody isn't nothin' now which doesn't hole up her cloz, and the hier you holes 'em the more you are notised."

Tax Levy Dialogue.

First Citizen (reading the city tax levy). Hillo! what in thunder is this item? "Wells and pumps" (for keeping the same in repair), $2,500.

Second Citizen—I thought such things were done away with in New York.

Third Citizen—I guess it must mean the expenses of the Croton Board. Of course we have no pumps.

First Citizen—No, no. The Croton Aqueduct Board asks for five thousand in another place. I don't understand it. "Pumps and wells"—it's a fraud. I'll write a letter to the *Herald* about it, right away. "Wells and pumps." Fiddlesticks!

Fourth Citizen—Now, don't go off half-cocked, my friend. The amount asked for is quite reasonable.

First Citizen—How so; where are our wells and pumps?

Fourth Citizen—I will enlighten you. We have a city government. Very good; in fact *well* and good. Is not the city treasury a *well;* and is not every office a *pump!*

First Citizen—Why necessarily a pump?

Fourth Citizen—Hath not each office a *sucker* in it? Therefore, I say the demand is reasonable. The wear and tear cannot be large, yet those suckers must not be allowed to get dry; hence the demand for repairs.

The citizens scatter, well convinced that they know but little about running a city goverment.

Taking it Easily.—Henrietta—I hear you are to be married; when is your wedding to come off?

Adelaide—O, I don't know, exactly; I have several visits to pay this spring, and one or two old flames to smother; besides, Harry says he cannot give up his shooting excursion this fall, and, as I shall be kept at Newport all summer—well, I guess we'll settle it about Christmas, when there is nothing else going on, you know.

What sort of legs does a factory mule go upon? Spindle-shanks, of course.

A Good Lighter.

In our regiments was a rollicking Irishman, called John, who had seen a vast deal of the world, and who had profited by his experience. John was favored with a face so grotesque and droll that his appearance among the boys was the signal for fun. The camp frontier was on the W—— turnpike, and here the boys congregated to amuse themselves after their own volition. John was usually among them, smoking vigorously, but talking little. One evening while here seated, there came up the road a certain commissary who, in some manner, had given offense to the men, and whom they howled and groaned at most unmercifully. At this the mule, upon which he was riding, took fright, and it was with great difficulty that the commissary could restrain him. Having accomplished this, and with many threats of direful import, he rode on, John only remarking that he was "a quare boy."

The following evening our friend again rode up gallantly, was again greeted as he had been the night before, and this time the mule threw him, in a sitting posture, on the ground· Picking himself up, he approached the men, swearing furiously, threatening that he would at once report the affair at headquarters and that they should be promptly and summarily dealt with. As he was about to move on, John, who had all this time maintained the utmost gravity, here broke in and addressed the discomfited commissary as follows :

"I say, Commissary, I don't know how good a rider ye are, but, begorra, ye're the divil at 'lightin' !" Amid a roar of laughter, our *ration-al* friend speedily got out of the way.

Avoid hypocrisy, my dear boys, in all its moods and tenses. If you think a man is a fool, tell him so, unless he is bigger than yourself.

"I have a great love for old *hymns*," said a pretty girl to her masculine companion. "I am much fonder of young *hers*," was his reply.

" 'Strate am de road. an narrow am de paff which leads off to glory !' Bredren—Blevers : You am sem-bled dis nite in comin' to hear de word, an' have it splained an' monstrated to yu ; yes yu is—an' I 'tend to splain it as de lite of libin day. We are all wicked sinners har below—it's a fack, bredren, an' l tell you how it cum. Yu see,

> " Adam was de fust man,
> Eve was de tudder ;
> Cane was de wicked man,
> Kase he killed his brudder."

Adam an Ebe were boff black men, an' so was Cane an' Able. Now I s'pose it seems to strike yer under-standings how de fust white man cum. Why, I let you know   Den you see when Cane killed his brud-der, de massa cum an' say, ' Cane, whar's yu brudder Able ?' Cane say, ' I don't know, massa.' But de nig-ger node all de time. Massa now get mad an' come again—speak mighty sharp dis time. ' Cane, whar's yu brudder Able, yu nigger ?' Cane now get frightened an' he turn white ; an' dis de way de fust white man cum upon dis earth. An' if it had not been for dat dar nigger Cane, we'd nebber been troubled wid de sassy whites 'pon de face of dis circumlar globe. De quire will sing de forty-eleventh hymn, tickler meter. Brud-der Joe, pass around the sassar."

Scientific men have recently discovered that the poi-son taken into the system from continual smoking of tobacco will cause death in one hundred and sixty seven years. We warn our readers who have been smoking nearly that time to break themselves of the habit at once.

"*Lookee here, mister,* I ain't complainin'; but this 'ere moosic stool you sold to my wife, we've twisted it roun' till we've twisted off un's ead, an' not a ha'porth o'toon can we get out of 'un."

Don't believe me, Sam? Why, I was dar all one winter.

What college was it?

Pale Ale College.

Yale College. What did you do?

Why, *I made all de fires* and cleaned de stugents' boots.

"What *is* this world coming to?" said a kind-hearted but simple old lady, as she threw down her newspaper. "Only to think," she continued, "that there in New York, at Fisk's Opera House, they allow a parcel of French dancing girls to *execute their grand pas* on the stage, with the people all a looking at 'em and applauding of 'em too!"

A physician going down street with a friend of his, said to him, "Let us avoid that pretty little woman you see there on the left; she recognizes me, and casts upon me looks of indignation. I attended her husband." "Ah! I understand, you had the misfortune to dispatch him." "On the contrary," replied the doctor, "I saved him, and she did not get a chance to get another."

Mrs. Jones (to her husband who has been "calling").—Well, Jones, you are a nice-looking man, ain't you? Where have you been?

Jones.—Been c-c-alling, my dear—hic!

Mrs. J.—I should say so; how came you so bedaubed with mud?

Jones.—Why, fac ish, I stumbled over a horse-car, and we fell into the mud together. (Jones is put to bed).

At Lawrence, Kansas, last Sunday, while a minister was holding forth in the church, a crowd got up a cock-fight in the yard. The people who had congregated to hear "the Word" went out to put a stop to the fight, but waited until the battle was over before objecting. The minister looked out of the window at the crowd and said: "We are all miserable sinners —which whipped?"

Life in Chicago.

Chicago Wife—What is the meaning of this, Henry ? We have been married nearly a whole year, and now you talk of getting a divorce, and have commenced to sell the furniture.

Chicago Husband—Yes, I am going to make a clean sweep and get an entire new domestic outfit. But you needn't take on so about it; your first husband didn't live with you but three months, and your second but six months, so I think I have done pretty well by you.

A young couple eloped from a neighboring town lately, and when at a safe distance from home were married. Soon after an officer was in pursuit, and upon arriving at the hotel where they were stopping he immediately entered their room and found them snug in bed. He explained his errand, when the young lady said, with a ringing laugh: "Tell ma it's too late. We've been married some time, and have been in bed half an hour. Snuggle up, George, and don't get out of bed for him."

Old Captain Moon (of Western steamboat notoriety,) was sitting one night on the capstan, keeping a sharp look-out ahead, when, lulled by the driving machinery, he went fast a-sleep, which was no sooner perceived, than one of the hands gave him a "turn round," facing the boiler fires, and then stuck a pin in him. Opening his eyes, he gave one jump and shouted: "Back her? stop her! here's a big steamboat right into us."

A marrying bachelor anxiously asks if it would be of any use to attempt to make love to a young lady after one has stood on her dress till he could hear the gathers rip at her waist? Yes, if you have a plenty of money, let her rip.

Instead of "hops" this season, we are to have round dances called "twists." It will be common to see a gentleman walk up to a lady, run out his elbow, and say "Madam, will you favor me with a twist?" and she twists.

New Mode of Borrowing Money.

Master.—Where have you been these few days past?

Clown.—I don't like to tell you, massa,

M.—Why not? Have you been fishing!

C.—He! he! he!

M.—Come, tell me.

C.—You won't be mad at me?

M.—No, sir.

C.—Well, I've been to jail.

M.—To jail?

C.—Yes, sir.

M.—What did they put you there for?

C.—For only borrowing two dollars and a half from a man.

M.—Why, sir, you're talking nonsense; people are not imprisoned for borrying money.

C.—Well, massa, you see I had to knock dis feller down tree or four times afore he let me hab it.

"What have you got that's good?" said a hungry traveller, as he seated himself at a dinner table in Salt Lake City. "Oh, we've got roast beef, corned beef, roast mutton, boiled and fried ham, and broiled curlews?" "What is curlew?" said the stranger. "Curlew! why curlew is a bird something like a snipe." "Could it fly?" "Yes." "Did it have wings?" "Yes." "Then I don't want any curlew. Anything that had wings and could fly, and didn't leave this d—d country, I don't want for dinner."

During the performance of an overture, one of the trumpets played too low, which the leader observing, he cried out: "Louder, louder!" No attention being paid, he repeated his command so often that at length the indignant Teuton threw down his trumpet in an agony of passion and exaustion, and turning to the audience exclaimed: "It is very easy to cry louder, louder! but vhere ist the vind to come from?"

Why is a sick Jew like a ruby?

Because it is a (jew ill.)

An Old, Old Story.

The following is as old as Luther, but is new to this generation at least. In the town of Kennebunk it was the custom, many years ago, for each family to take turns in killing their hogs, so that, by distribution, all could have fresh pork the season round. One individual, who had enjoyed his roast pork, and pork and beans, having had many of the like favors showered thick upon him, thought it no more than right that he should return the compliment to his neighbors. Meeting a neighbor, Mr. Gill by name, he told him that he thought he should reciprocate ; but the great trouble was, his pork was only a " little pig," and would not go half round the village. " Well," said Gill, " I'll tell you what to do; you just kill the pesky critter and hang him outside your barn, so that the people will see it, and at twelve o'clock to night you just come out and take him in, and swear somebody stole him—do you see ?" " Jess so !" says the other ; and straightway slaughtered his pig, and hung him in view of all passers-by. At about mid-night he went to take his defunct squealer in, when behold, it was missing ! He went to bed, troubled in mind and body, but on rising next morning went straightway to find Gill, and the following conversation took place :

Mr. J.—"Gill, my friend, by the powers, my pig, that I killed yesterday, was stolen last night !"

Mr. G.—" You don't say so ?—goodness me !"

Mr. J.—" Yes ; I hung it out on the barn, and when I went to take it in, I found it gone."

Mr. G.—" That's the way ! keep it up—keep it up ! If I did not know you were lying, I'd swear you told the truth !"

Mr. J.—" But I tell you, confound ye! I'm telling the truth. My pig was stole !"

Mr. G.—" That's it! How wonderful! You beat the best actor I've ever seen ! It's a big joke !"

Mr. J.—" But, hang it, it's no joke to me ! The pig was stolen last night, and that's Gospel truth !"

Mr. G.—" Well, if you tell all the village with such an earnest manner, every man, woman, and child will surely believe ye."

Mr. J.—" But I tell you—well, no matter."

And Mr. J. left his friend Gill with curses loud and deep. It transpired that Gill was the cruel one who stole the little pig away.

Difficulties in Either Case.—One evening, at a private party at Oxford, at which Dr. Johnson was present, a recently published essay on the future life of brutes was referred to, and a gentleman, disposed to support the author's opinion that the lower animals have an " immortal part," familiarly remarked to the doctor, " Really, sir, when we see a very sensible dog, we don't know what to think of him." Johnson, turning quickly round, replied, " True, sir ; and when we see a very foolish fellow, we don't know what to think of him."

Metaphor.—Sometimes the sayings of colored folks will provoke laughter in spite of one's self. Last winter, during a revival in a negro congregation at Harmer, one of the members—an old and very earnest Christian woman—relating her experience and rejoicing in the fact that she was a Christian woman, said : "I would rather be a deck-hand on de ark of de Lord dan be de Captain ob de Wild Wagoner." The Wild Wagoner was then the Wheeling and Cincinnati packet, and one of the finest vessels above the falls of the Ohio.

" Is my face dirty ?" asked a young lady from the backwoods, while seated with her aunt at the dinner table on a steamboat running from Cairo to New Orleans. " Dirty ! No. Why did you ask ?" " Because that insulting waiter insists upon putting a towel beside my plate. I've thrown three under the table, and yet every time he comes around he puts another one before me."

Sixty skaters have been drowned in Ohio within the past two weeks. The undertakers indorse skating as a rational amusement.

Awful.

" So you had a suicide at your house last week ?"

" Oh, yes siree, and de affair almost scart me to deff."

" Who was the person ?"

" A German from California."

" Did he come by the steamer ?"

" No, he cum ober de Erecipilus by de Nicerauger route and stopped at our house prebious to his 'ribal."

" Was he insane ?"

" I don't know, Sam, but I thought he was crazy by his actions."

" Why so ?"

" Coz he gib me a shillin' de minute he laid eyes on me—and from dat minute I stuck to him for fear dat somebody would rob him."

" How did you discover the deed ?"

" Why de next mornin de chambermaid was goin up stairs and she had to pass by dis gemman's door ; and just as she got to de door she smelt lodlum, and when she smelt lodlum she smelt a rat. She knocked at de door—but no answer—den she broke de door down and dar she beheld— "

" What ?"

" De California man layin on de floor wid his boots on and in his troat was stickin a lodlum bottle."

" What did she then do ?"

" Why, sent right away for de Sturgeon."

" The Surgeon, you mean."

" Yes ; he come and made a desission here in de neck."

" Incision, you mean."

" Yes ; right nigh de borax, which reached as fur as de equilibrium into de sarcophigus, and puttin a cortven into de desission, gib him a poke into de dispotchlus, when out flew de bottle and was safe."

" What—the man ?"

" No—de bottle, to be sure."

Why are soldiers apt to be tired in the month of April ?   Because they've just gone through a MARCH ?

New Rat Exterminator.

" Massa, I've jest discovered how to catch rats a new way."

" How do you mean ?"

" What will you gib me to tell you ?"

" Nothing."

" Well, neber mind ; you've known me a long time, and so hab I known you a long time, and so I'll tell you for nofin'."

" Well, how do you catch rats your way ?"

" Listen. Git a nice piece ob cheese—go to your bed-room—say your prayers—git into bed—den *eat* your cheese—lay on yer back—keep still, wid your mouth wide open—and pooty soon de rats will smell de cheese. Fust dey'll hunt down round de floor—den under de bed, and at last git on de bed. Den you must keep awful still, or you'll frighten 'em away. Dey approach yer mouth, dey look in, den go away. Dey come back—den dey put der tail into your mouth to see how deep it is. Dey prepare to *go in*. Der mustachers tickle your mouth, the *ears* are past your lips. Now's your time—*Bite !* and you got 'em."

At a railway station in the Black Country the other day, an altercation occurred between the station-master and a huge collier, the occupant of a third-class carriage.

" You must pay for the dog, I tell you," said the station-master, pointing to a fine specimen of the bull type, which sat, bandy-legged and blinking serenely, beneath the seat.

" I sho', ' returned the collier, curtly.

" Then he must come out," rejoined the station-master.

" Fotch him out, then."

The dog, seeming to understand it all, seconded his master's invitation by a slight lifting of the upper lip and a wicked gleam of his eyes. He went on by that train, and no fare was paid for him.

When is a boat like a knife ?

When it's a cutter.

Frailty, thy Name is Woman!

Mrs. A.—I say, Mary, there are those two men who have followed us all over the Park; let us call a policeman.

Mary—No, no, don't do anything of the kind. One of them is that model husband of mine (the man who never has eyes for any woman but me). He does not know me with my new suit on. Don't look around; it might spoil the dear fellow's sport.

"I stood near a beautiful girl last night, so pure and white and delicate that *she seemed to foam up over her stays* like another goddess born of the sea; and my mind would morbidly follow a cream through the coral mouth and pearly teeth, down the dark passage of the throat, to—" Oh, Don Piatt, how could you?

Milburn, the blind preacher, is making so much money lecturing that several other ministers are wondering why they couldn't have been born without eyes, that they might go it blind.

"Do you know a horse from a jackass, when you see them?" asked a brow-beating barrister of a rather dull-looking witness. "Oh, ye-as, just so," drawled out the intended victim, gazing intently at his legal tormenter; "I knows the difference; and I'd never take you for a horse."

"Are these pure canaries?" asked a young gentleman who was negotiating for a gift for his fair one. "Yes, sir," said the dealer confidently; "I raised them 'ere birds from canary seed."

An illiterate farmer wishing to enter some animals at an agricultural exhibition, wrote as follows to the secretary of the society: "Also enter me for the best jackass. I am sure of getting the prize."

Not difficult to Please.—"I always sing to please myself," said a gentleman, who was humming a tune in company. "Then you're not at all difficult to please," said a lady who sat next him.

Back Bone.

Our friend Jenks was at the late yacht race in our harbor, and resolving to show his Yankee back bone and knowledge of ship building generally, he interviewed Mr. Ashbury, of the *Cambria*. Here is his account of it :

The *Cambria* was lying in the stream, and with the noble disregard for private rights characteristic of all true Americans, we boarded her. We found her fast aground on the h's which the crew had inconsiderately dropped overboard. Mr. Ashbury was aboard, and we had quite a pleasant and intelligent conversation with him regarding the different build of American and British yachts. He thinks we build our vessels too narrow in the beam and with too much drag aft. "Mr. Ashbury," I remarked, " can you conscientiously say on your word as a British sailor that you think the main chains of a fore-and-aft rigged vessel should be on a line with the cat-head, instead of standing flush with the lanyards of the main shifter—perhaps a trifle abaft rather than forward, but certainly not on a dead line with either of the companion ways of the starboard gangway?" He said conscientiously he could not. " Then, sir," I said, you confess the proud pre-eminence of Yankee ship building, and mark me, sir, boast of proud Britain as you may, long after your tarry top-lights are shivered, and your top-gallant eyebrows are crumbling in the dust, the American jackstay will float proudly at the taffrail of civilization !"

And with that I hitched up my trousers, and came away.

Sir Charles Napier once asked a fellow, black as a chimney-sweep, " if a coal-pit would spoil his clothes ?"

" Bless you, I goes down ten times a day, and never minds my clothes," was the answer.

What is the legal-tender act? Kissing your own wife—kissing your neighbor's wife is an illegal tender act.

Laughing.

" Massa, did you eber try fur to make anybody laugh ?"

"No, sir, I never did."

" Well now, dare's great many ways to make folks laugh, sich as pokin straws into dar ears, makin faces at 'em, and a great many oder ways too numerical fur to mention ;—but I kin tell you a sure and sartin way ob my own inwention."

" And pray in what manner can you force people to laugh ?"

" Listen—

He dat would move anoder man to laughter,
Must first begin—'toder comes soon arter."

A young man in Louisville examined a keg of damaged gunpowder with a red-hot poker to see if it was good. It is believed by his friends that he has gone to Europe although a man has found some human bones and a piece of shirt-tail about twenty miles from Louisville.

A family at New Haven, after building a fire one morning, heard a noise and found the cook-stove had been blown all over the house. They don't say much about it, but the man next door thinks his coal lasts longer than it did before he put a charge of powder into a large lump.

A New Soup.—A dandy, remarking one summer day that the weather was so excessively hot, that when he put his head in a basin of water it fairly boiled, received for reply—"Then, sir, you have a calf's head soup at very little expense."

A cotemporary says : " Don't marry dimples, nor ankles, nor eyes, nor mouths, nor hair, nor necks, nor chins, nor teeth, nor simpers. These bits and scraps of femininity are mighty poor things to tie to. Marry the true thing." Now, who's been fooling around this editor with such things as these? Poor fellow, if he only lived in Indiana!

Taking the Census.

"Sam, you know I always tell you my secrets?"

"Yes, you do, Julius, and by this time I should think you had none left."

"Yes, I have, though."

"Julius, let me hear it. It must be good for the keeping so long."

"No, Sam, somewhat spilt; but I'll tell you if you won't tell nobody else."

"Certainly not."

"Well, Sam, I was out takin de census de oder day, an' I cum 'cross a house what had a nice scent of broiled ham a-cumin out ob de chinks ob de shutters; so I stepped up to de house an axed——"

"What, asked the house?"

"No, a young lady dat came to de door as I was takin de satistical census ob manufactures an products —'if dere was any produce raised here last year.'"

"What did she say?"

"She sed, 'Yes, sir; I've one 'bout six months old!'"

"What did she mean, Julius?"

"Go 'long wid you!"

"Well, what did you do?"

"I left."

"Why?"

"Case 'twas time."

Old Women.

"Sam, who is de oldest woman?"

"I don't know, Julius."

"I do, Sam,"

"Who was she?"

"Aunty-Quity; an I know anoder one nearly as old."

"Who was she?"

"Aunty-Deluvian."

"But, Julius, did you live cotemporary with those women?"

"No; but my mudder did."

"What was your mother's maiden name, Julius?"

"No, it wasn't Julius; it was Aunty-Past."

A Feeling Judge.—An individual having been con-
victed upon rather slight evidence, before a judge in
Hagarstown, Md., he proceeded to pass judgment as
follows:

"Prisoner at the bar! You have been found guilty
by a jury of your countrymen of a crime which sub-
jects you to the penalty of death. You say you are
innocent; the truth of that assertion is only known to
yourself and God. It is my duty to leave you for
execution. If guilty, you richly deserve the fate which
awaits you—if innocent, it will be a gratification to
feel that you were hanged without such a crime on your
conscience. In either case you will be delivered from
a world of care."

Not Drunk by a Darned Sight!—"Mrs. Smithers,
where's my (hic cup) shavings 'tensils?"

"Your shaving utensils? What do you want of
your shaving utensils at this hour of the night? Come
to bed, you brute, you're drunk."

"You lie, my love, I'm not (hic cup) drunk; but I
want to know what come (hic cup) of that blue eyed
bonnet what wore the white silk young 'oman. Say,
where's them shaving 'tensils? If you don't speak,
(hic cup) I'll take a door, my love, and burst the club
in."

When we left, Smithers was talking about the Con-
stitution to the key hole of a bed-room door.

A Child of Erin.—Deacon C. had an Irish girl who
was decidedly verdant. The deacon was building a
woodhouse on ground which inclosed a well.

"And, sure," said the Milesian help, "are ye going
to move the well?" Observing a smile on his face, she
added, "Ah! what a big fool I be. Sure every drop
of wather would run out movin' it!"

A Western paper, speaking of Olive Logan's lecture,
says: "She removed the mystery which surrounded
the girls." What? and half the audience men! naughty
Logan.

State Overseer.

"Sam, did you ever know any mean man?"

"Yes; I knew a man once so mean that his shadow wouldn't follow him.'

"No, that wasn't it, Sam. He was afraid his shadow might ax him for somethin'."

"My father was better than your father. My father was bigger dan your father."

"Don't know your father."

"Because, if my father cared for your father, when your father was wid my fader. Whose afraid of your father? Say!"

"Now he was a mean man."

"That's a scandalous fact."

"What did he die of?"

"Enlargement of the heart."

"Where?"

"At the White House."

"No; the poor-house."

"I suppose he drove his own carriage?"

"Drove an omnibus."

"Has he ever been to Europe?"

"Yes, indeed! He's been to the States Prison, too."

"Been to the States Prison?"

"Yes; he had a situation there for six months."

"What kind of a situation!"

"He was overseer?"

"What did he oversee?"

"Why, he looked over the walls every day to see if there was any chance to get out."

A Parisian play-writer meets a critic on the street, and "interviews" him on the subject of several harsh criticisms he has written on a piece of his. "Sir, you are condemning my play in unmeasured terms, while you yourself would not be able to write a single scene of it!" "Excuse me, sir," replied the polite critic with an urbane smile, "but a jury sitting in judgment on an offender is not exactly required to have committed the crime the accused is being tried for."

A Genius.

"Massa, did you know dat I was a great painter!"

"No, sir, I was not aware of it."

"O yes, sir, I is."

"What was the last subject you portrayed on canvas?"

"What did you say, sir?"

"What was the last thing you painted?"

"A horse and cart."

"Was it natural?"

"Natural!—guess it was. Why, I'd no sooner got de traces put on de hoss, dan he drew me all round de town."

"Wonderful! Have you anything more of equal wonder to tell me?"

"Yes, sir, I'm an inwenter, too."

"What have you ever invented?"

"Suspenders."

"Suspenders? And what material difference have you made in them?"

"A great deal of difference. De suspenders I've inwented is constructed on such a plan dat when you come to a stream ob water dey lift you right ober on de oder side."

There are several ways of showing gallantry. The street-car conductors in Wilmington, N. C., when the mud is deep, provide a pair of high boots which they hang upon the break behind, and when a lady passenger wishes to alight or to get on board, they offer them their choice in getting through the usual foot of mud which paves the streets (after the fashion of our own Fifth avenue, only more of it), either to slip on the boots or allow the conductor to carry them to the curb stone. Some of them also provide stilts, but the conductors are happy to state that a majority of the pretty, unmarried ones prefer to be carried over. Who wouldn't work for two dollars a day on such a road?

A Stingy Company.

The Captain Watt A. Lyre of the following story is fictitious in name only. The narrator of the Munchausenisms therein contained, and of others equally as absurd and ridiculous, was alive, but a very old man, only a few years ago.

This story, and others which may follow, have their sole aim and use in illustrating the long-bow proclivities of here and there one among a generation which is rapidly passing away. Many of my readers, as they recall the odd stories of some of the old grandfathers of the past, will fully understand what I mean.

One of the queerest of the many queer stories that Captain Watt A. Lyre used to relate was the following, illustrating him as a skatist :

"Speakin' of skatin'," said the old man, " if there ever was a place where I really felt tew hum it was on a pair of skates. Nobody in my part of the kentry had any business with me there, I tell you. A mile a minute wus my usual gait, and that without pullin' out any of my extra pegs either.

"'Minidab Pollard and I were out one day— in the winter of '25 I guess it wus. It was cold. We hadn't skated twenty miles afore our breaths were friz more'n eighteen inches long behind us.

"I found I'd got tew let out a link tew keep warm. I let it out 'cordingly, tew the tune of some eighteen or twenty rod at a lick, and in less'n three minutes, though 'Minidab was a desprit good skater, he looked like a bumblee on the ice away behind me.

"I had my head down tew keep the sharp wind from cuttin' my face, and so belted away without thinkin' a single word of the big dam across the river, right ahead of me.

"I got within two or three rod of the 'tarnal thing afore I seen it at all. I was goin' straight for a forge that stood clus up tew and partly under the right hand eend of it.

"I tried tew turn, but I might jest as well have sot out tew put britchin' on tew a streak of lightnin'. My left heel-strap broke, over I went head fust, and down through the shop winder, plum between a monstrous big chunk of red-hot iron and a trap-hammer that was poundin' ontew it at the rate of ten clips to the second. And I didn't scorch a hair nor raise a single black and blue spot on me nuther.

"The plaguey hammer cum down so clus behind, though, that it tuck off about six inches of my right coat-tail pocket.

"But I didn't keer much for that. It wus an old coat, and there wus nothin' but a plug of terbacker in the pocket.

"I paid for the winder I split and thought that wus the eend on't. But it warn't. Three days afterward, that mean, stingy company was small enough tew send me another bill for jest six cents.

"They had found a flaw in the chunk of iron, where the plug of terbacker and piece of coat tail had got stamped in, and they wanted some damages on that, tew."

A citizen of Cedar Falls, Iowa, had such faith in a chemical fire-engine that he set fire to a house just for the fun of putting it out. He charged on the fire with his machine, when it refused to squirt, and the house went right on burning and wouldn't wait. You can buy that engine for fifty cents on a dollar. Perhaps that man ain't sick. He writes us that he has bought a hen and will attend to legitimate business hereafter.

A new beauty in kerosene has just been discovered in Boston. A man there caught a rat the other day and after soaking him nicely with the article and setting it gently on fire, he let him go among his companions, as a sort of a hint of what was in store for them if they did not vamoose his shebang. He says it occurred to him what a mistake he had made the moment he saw the flames coming up through the floor.

The Question.

"Julius what's de worst feeliug you ever 'sperienced ?"
" Mortification."

" At what time did that happen ?"

" When 1 popped de question to a gal and she said No."

A rich scene was witnessed in the gentleman's cabin of a Jersey City ferry-boat the other morning. A boy about thirteen years old sat quietly smoking a cigar, enjoying the weed with the air of a veteran. He held a large bundle across his arm, one end resting on the floor. The cabin was crowded. A gentleman who sat next to the urchin was apparently very much annoyed by the-careless manner in which the upper end of the bundle was continually thrust under his nose. He called the attention of the boy to the fact two or three times, and at last, losing all patience, exclaimed in a loud tone :

" What in thunder have you got in that infernal bundle ?"

Coolly taking the cigar out of his mouth and holding it at an elevation which brought the lighted extremity directly under and within an inch of the bundle, he replied with the utmost nonchalance :

" Skyrocket—!"

The curious gentleman gave one look at the fellow, and springing hastily from his seat, shouting. "We shall all be blowed up !" beat a precipitate retreat to the deck.

With a sly wink Young America turned to the other passengers in the vicinity, who were in a state of consternation, and observed quietly :

" Skyrocket-sticks : the old cove got a scare for nothing." .

The laugh that followed convinced the " old cove," who was looking for the anticipated explosion at a safe distance from the cabin door, that he had been sold.

Why is a nail-post in the wall like an old man ?
Because its in-firm ?

Definitions.

"Sass fur de goose is sass fur de gander."—De culinary adornments which suffice fur de female ob de race anser, kin be relished also wid de masculine adult ob de same species.

" Let well 'nuff alone."—Suffer a healthy sufficiency to remain by itself.

" It's an ill wind dat blows nobody any good." Dat gale is truly diseased dat puffeth benefaction to nonenity.

" A stitch in time sabes nine."—De fust impression ob a needle on a rent obviateth a nine-fold introduction.

Speaking of the young men of Washington, a lady who knows whereof she speaks, says :

" You don't know half. The youths you noticed are the society men here, and are used by the mothers and daughters as so many conveniences. Do you know that when acting as escort to the opera, for example, they are furnishing these beaux not only with tickets, but carriages? They are put to no expense save for gloves and neckties. After a while these even will be furnished the harmless innocents. The mother, for example, addresses the following note to the proposed escort :

"'My dear Mr. Lillypup :

"'We find ourselves in possession of a box at the opera to-night, but Mr. Ball is so busy he can not spare time for such a luxury. May we count on you to escort us?

"'Yours sincerely,' etc.

" And now when one of these properties of society invites a lady to a reception, ball, or party, he is expected to meet her at the dressing-room, and afterwards help her to her carriage. The young man is run on the most economical principles."

We are glad to hear this. Let them be made useful, for many of them are government officials, and should be made to do something.

Two Amiable Neighbors.

A French paper tells the following good story : The bedchambers of two wealthy gentlemen, who belong to different social circles, are adjacent, and as is usual now-a-days, thin partititions divide them. One spends his nights at his club-house, never returning before half-past five in the morning. His neighbor rises at six and sits down at once to his piano, which he does not quit till dinner. The former complained to the Commissary of Police, who laughed in his face, and told him to keep better hours. As he had a lease for six years he could not change his apartment. He thought of sending a challenge to his neighbor; his neighbor was paralyzed in the lower limbs. He had his wall lined with thick hair mattresses; still the "sharps" penetrated into his room. He made his servants play the French horn—his neighbor had him fined by the police ; the French horn cannot be played except during the *jours gras*. He made his servants take a hammer and rap against the wall—his neighbor waited until he was tired, and then began to play. He then bought a hand-organ, which was sadly out of tune, and ordered a turn-spit which would turn eight days without being wound up, and which he had fitted to the organ. The turn-spit was put in motion, after it and the organ had been placed next the chamber wall. The piano player bore the organ for nineteen hours ; at the end of that time he sent a letter of truce ; he was told the club hunter had gone out of town, and wouldn't be back for a week. The pianist sold his lease—the organ is still going.

The illicit distilleries of Brooklyn appear to be doing a thriving business—brewing trouble for their proprietors and the revenue collectors. The " worm " of the still appears to be bent on not keeping still, or at least it is very suggestive of the worm that dieth not (if our scripture hasn't wholly gone back on us). It seems utterly impossible to instill into some poison-makers a whole-some regard for the law, and the only way left for Uncle Sam is to " worm " it out of them.

That's What's the Matter.—A steward on an Ohio River steamer was addressed by an uneasy and excited individual, who wanted him to put somebody off the boat. The candidate for a forcible disembarkation was pointed out, but the steward could see nothing out of the way. "You don't, eh? Don't you see a man sitting there hugging a woman?" "Well, yes," replied the steward; "but what of that? hasn't a fellow a right to embrace his wife?" "That's just what I want to run him out for," replied the stranger, dancing around; "that's my wife, and I have stood it so long that I've got mad!"

A sharp man stopped at a Boston hotel and got supper and lodging, agreeing to kill all the rats on the premises to pay for his entertainment. In the morning the landlord asked him to go in and kill the rats, when the guest asked for an ax, after obtaining which, he said: "Fetch on your rats, Mr. Landlord." He hadn't agreed to catch the rats, don't you see? Can't get much ahead of these Bosting chaps.

An enthusiastic admirer of the beauties of beautiful women recently startled a friend: "Been to church this morning, he asserted. "To church?" "Yes, and such necks! full and white, and good enough to eat— six of them all in a row; watched them all through service. Oh, my, what necks!"

In Ohio a merchant sent a dunning letter to a man, who replied by return mail: "You say you are holding my note yet. That is all right—perfectly right. Just keep holding on to it, and if you find your hands slipping, spit on them, and try again. Yours affectionately."

Where it Came From.—A lady, whose fondness for generous living had given her a flushed face and rubicund nose, consulted Dr. Cheyne. Upon surveying herself in the glass, she exlaimed, "Where, in the name of wonder, doctor, did I get such a nose as this?" "Out of the decanter, madam," replied the doctor.

A young man of twelve years, in an Illinois town, laid a train of powder through the kitchen and touched it off to have some fun with his mother. The old lady was discovered in the act of going out of the window, head first. The second scene was the middle of the boy and the old lady's shoe " playing tag."

Since it has transpired that the minister Cooke took the girl to Philadelphia and left her alone all night, many of his congregation are justly indignant. They say that was no way to use a girl, and, indeed, they may be more than half right.

Brigham Young regrets the million and a half of women that are " wasted," as he terms it, in this country, by being unmarried. It is sad, and he so young and willing with his saving grace.

Mr. Big says, and Big knows, that the position of physician's bill collector is a difficult calling. It may not require any great ability, but there is no employment which requires constant *application*.

There must be good shooting out in Utah. A friend of ours who has just returned from there says that the grasshoppers are so large and so numerous out that way, that they have eaten up every thing green, and are now loafing around waiting for the potatoes to get ripe enough to dig. How is that for insects?

Moses says he wishes he could hear of some place where people never die; he would go and end his days there. Moses is the same eccentric individual who, attending divine service in a church where the people came very late to a meeting, observed that it seemed to be the fashion there "for nobody to go to meeting till after everybody got there."

It is said that husbands are so scarce in Massachusetts that the girls are actually taking up with lawyers. What became of those Chinese shoemakers? Are they exhausted?

An Iowa John lately courted and engaged to marry a young girl, who, in a miff at some neglect on John's part, revenged herself by marrying Isaac, John's father. John countered by marrying the mother of his recent betrothed—John becoming the step-father of his own step-mother, while Isaac's wife was compelled to become the daughter-in-law of her own step-son. And thus John became his own grandfather by brevet.

A chap out West, who had been severely afflicted with the palpitation of the heart, says he found instant relief by the application of another palpitating heart. Another triumph of homeopathy. "Like cures like."

An Ohio lady seeks a divorce on the ground of a want of tenderness on her husband's part. He hammered her with an ax-helve for over three-quarters of an hour, and then triumphantly inquired of her, "How is that for high?"

Music Hath Charms.—One of the best things to resist fatigue with is music. Girls who "could not walk a mile to save their lives," will dance, in company with a knock-kneed clarionet and superannuated fiddle, from tea-time till sunrise.

Some New York paper started a sensation story, with no truth in it, about a new species of bug that had been discovered in the street cars, with horns and things, that was poisonous as a rattlesnake, and now a Philadelphia paper comes out and claims that they have had them all the time. You can't get ahead of those Quakers much, with your stories.

A friend says he lately cured his daughter of a severe attack of the Grecian Bend by compelling her to drink two bottles of mucilage and then lashing her securely to a small sapling. He says that the only trouble was that she didn't have stiffening enough in her back to keep herself perpendicular, and so when the mucilage got set she was found to be all right.

It was reported in Williamsport, Penn., among the *élite*, that one of the upper ten was in the habit of beating his wife, and a committee of old ladies were deputed to wait upon her, and learn the facts from her own lips. They did so, and to their horror learned that he was in the habit of beating her, " but," remarked the lady, " it is at euchre !" The committee mizzled.

We heard a Dutchman the other evening give vent to the following :

" Now, every poty he say something pout me, vat ish my country. Now vot you dink I ish ?"

" Why, you are an American, of course; that is plain ;" said his auditor, swallowing the remainder of his lager.

" Yah ! yah ? yah ! dat ish all recht ! I fools more ash a hundred beeples dat vay."

A rich organ-grinder has just died in San Francisco who has left a large fortune to his monkey. It is said that the dear creature has become a great favorite with unmarried women in that region, and if one of them should marry him for his money it would not be the first case on record where a woman had married a monkey from money considerations.

A widow woman at Nashua, Iowa, who allowed her only child to play with a six-shooter, is frequently heard to sing " Who Will Care for Mother Now ? They buried him at eventide.

Indiana is agitating the question of revising the divorce laws, so as to make divorces harder to obtain. That will be the best thing they can do to get rid of surplus population.

Three burglars worked twenty-four hours on a county safe in Wisconsin, and only got three cents, and now they have presented a bill against the county for obtaining labor under false pretences.

At a wedding at Layfayette, Ind., the choir sung " Come, ye Disconsolate," The bride said if the people would wait until the ceremony was over, she would put a mansard roof on the head of the leader.

" A down-cast " Yankee has recently invented a rat exterminator, consisting of a sort of powder snuff. The animal jerks his head off at the *third sneeze!*

Two friends, some years married and widely separated, lately exchanged telegrams thus : " To ——. All well. We have two pair of twins. How is that for high ?" "To ——. We have three little girls. Three of a kind beats two pair !"

Query by an outsider. It has been evident for a long time that France could not work against Prussia. Why ? Because France surrendered her only Toul (tool).

A rich Philadelphia contractor, in a severe fit of the gout, told his physician he suffered the pains of the damned. The doctor coolly answered, " What, already !"

A paper in Wisconsin says that the Board of Education in that State has resolved to erect a building large enough to accomodate five hundred students three stories high.

A young lady in Oshkosh was lately presented with an elegant card case from one of her admirers. A few days afterward, while showing it to a lady friend, she remarked that " she wished he had given her a larger one. This little thing won't hold more than half a deck."

A Kansas lady, on retiring to her room, found it literally filled with martins, which had flown in during her absence. Instead of turning them out into the cold, the kind hearted lady captured nearly all the little creatures and had them served up the next day in a pot pie.

Lot of Conundrums.

Why will the monsters of the deep be better posted than the cable operators?

Because they *nose* the news before it reaches either side.

Why are sheep the most dissipated and unfortunate of animals?

Because they *gambol* in their youth, frequent the turf, and are always fleeced.

Why is a hen on a fence like a cent?

Because there's a head on one side and a tail on the other.

Why is a dandy like a venison steak?

Because he is a bit of a buck.

Why is a philanthropist like a good horse?

Because he always stops at the word woe (whoa).

Why are ladies like bells?

Because you can never find out their metal until you have given them a ring.

Why is a *precarious* bank note like an impenitent sinner?

Because it don't know that its 'redeemer' liveth."

Why is General Scott like a stack of wheat?

Because he was never thrashed.

Why is a street-door like a barrel of Whisky?

Because it is frequently *tapped*.

Why is justice like a shad?

Because she carries scales.

Why is a certain game of cards like economy?

Because its seven up (*savin' up*.)

Why does a horse never starve in harness?

Because he always has a bit in his mouth.

Why are inn-keeper's wives like Generals?

Because they are rulers of hosts.

When is a door more than a door?

When it is to (*two.*)

Why is the medical profession the most tedious?

Because it requires more patience (*patients*) than any other.

" I travel on my good looks," said a young lady of the period. "Then you will never be found far from home," replied a rejected lover.

" I am going to the post-office, John; shall I inquire for you?" " Well, yes, if you have a mind to, but I don't think you will find me there."

An old lady in Indiana keeps a flock of seventy or eighty ganders, whose soft warblings and plumage are her delight. What a goose *she* must be.

We understand that the postage on papers is reduced to one cent. Well, of course, there will be two sent where there is one-sent now, and so that will make it even.

An urchin being sent for five cents' worth of maccaboy snuff, forgot the name of the article, and asked for five cents' worth of make-a-boy sneeze.

" The man who raised a cabbage-head has done more good than all the metaphysicians," said a stump orator at a meeting. " Then," said a wag, " your mother ought to have taken the premium."

" O, mother," said a very little child, " Mr. S—— does love aunt Lucy—he sits by her, he whispers to her, and he *hugs* her." " Why, Edward, your aunt does not suffer that, does she?" " Suffer it! yes, mother—she *loves* it."

Things are pretty evenly divided, after all. The poor man has no money, while the rich man has no appetite. The former lives in dread of the alms-house, and the latter of dyspepsia and white pine pudding. Who's ahead?

A young man at La Crosse, Wis., looked through the key-hole of a girls bed-room, and ever since the doctors have been trying to get a knitting-needle out of the place where his north eye used to be.

Derivation of Buss.—Buss—to kiss. Rebuss—to kiss again. Blunderbuss—two girls, kissing each other. Omnibus—to kiss all the girls in the room.

Philosophy says that shutting the eyes makes the sense of hearing more acute. A wag suggests that this accounts for the many closed eyes which are seen in our churches every Sunday.

Pontiac lawyers of the earlier class were not usually caught napping, and were proverbially full of expedients. One of the sharpest of these found himself cornered before a justice one day, and was forced to recite a repealed act.

His opponent was on his track, and read the repealing act.

"I knew very well," said the exhibitor of the read law, "that the letter of this law had been repealed, but I insist, if the Court please, that the spirit remains."

The Court thought so, too, and gave judgment accordingly.

A milkman accounted for the thinness of his milk by saying that the cows got caught in the rain.

Henry Clay used to say that there were three classes of persons with whom it was never safe to quarrel.

"First, ministers—for the reason they had pulpits from which they could denounce me, and I had none from which to reply.

"Secondly, editors—for they had the most powerful engines, from which they could every day hurl wrath and fury upon me, and I had none through which to reply.

"And finally, with women—for they would have the last word anyhow."

Receipt for finding a husband—More common sense and less wit.

More useful occupation, and less music.

More study of the mysteries of the kitchen, and less of the mysteries of Paris.

More proof to men that they will find in their wife a helpmate, and not embarrassment.

This receipt, if thoroughly tried, will greatly lessen the number of bachelors.

Old lady to a hackman—"But these hacks are dangerous. You never know who rides in them. We might get the small pox."

Coachee—"You've no cause to be afeard of my coach, mum, for I've had the hind wheel waccinated, and it took beautiful."

An Irish magistrate, censuring some boys for loitering in the street, argued, "If everybody were to stand in the street, how could anybody get by ?"

A poor man, who was ill, being asked by a gentleman whether he had taken any remedy, replied :

"No, I aint taken any remedy, but I've taken lots of physic."

Rowland Hill was in the habit of taking nearly everything he saw or heard into the pulpit, and using it in his sermons. When preaching on the government of the temper, he said :

"I once took tea with an old lady, who was very particular about her china. The servant, unfortunately, broke the best bread-and-butter plate ; but her mistress took very little notice of the circumstance at the time, only remarking :

" 'Never mind, Mary ; accidents cannot be avoided.'

" 'My word, but I shall have it by-and-by,' said the girl, when she got out of the room.

"And so it turned out. The old lady's temper was corked up for a season, but it came out with a terrible vengeance when the company had retired."

A celebrated divine, who prided himself upon the originality of his sermons, was once told, jocularly, that a sermon he had preached was excellent.

"But," said the wag who told him, "I had previously read every word of it in a book I have at home."

The astonished clergyman begged for a sight of the volume.

"Oh, I have no doubt you have the same book in your library ; it is 'Webster's Dictionary'!"

A Mistaken Goose.—A Western paper tells the following story respecting a gallant widower who resides at Holly Springs, Mississippi, and who, it was said, had been casting the sheep's eye of affection at a certain amiable " vidder " in the neighborhood, although others thought his visits were covertly paid to the " vidder's darters." Be this how it may, one evening he called as usual, and found the family party hard to work upon some garments of cloth. The girls were sewing, and the widow was pressing the seams. The widower " hung up his hat," and, as usual, took his seat by the fire; just at that moment it happened that the widow had done with the pressing iron (vulgo tailor's goose ;) she set it down on the hearth, and called to her negro man in a loud voice—" Jake! Jake! come and take out this goose !"

The widower started up in astonishment, not knowing what to make of this abrupt order.

" Jake, do you hear ?" again exclaimed the widow.

" I beg your pardon, Mrs. M.," said the widower, with visible agitation, " but pray don't call Jake—if you wish me to leave your house I will go at once without the interference of servants." The ladies roared with laughter, and it took some moments to explain to the chagrined widower his mistake. He has not been known to visit the widow M. since that memorable night.

A Sweet Boy.—A little boy hearing his father say, "There is a time for all things," climbed up behind his mother's chair, and whispering in her ear, asked, " When was the proper time for hooking sugar out of the sugar bowl."

Windy.—Sentimental Young Lady.—" Pray, Mr. Charles, how is the wind ?"

Embarrassed Young Gentleman. — " Pretty well thank you, ma'am."

Keep your countenance open and your thoughts shut

We believe it is rare that an editor indulges in a drop, but when they do, their readers are sure to find it out. A contemporary was called upon to record a "melancholy event" at a time when his head was rather heavy, and did it after the following manner:

"Yesterday morning, at four o'clock P. M., a man with a heel in the hole of his stocking, committed arsenic by swallowing suicide. The inquest of the verdict returned a jury that the deceased came to the facts in accordance with his death. He leaves a child and six small wives to lament the end of his untimely loss. In death we are in the midst of life."

Here is a bona-fide incident which transpired in town lately:

A colored woman, one of the converts during the recent revival, had an altercation with a sable youth employed in the same house, and was interrupted in her lively tirade by the mistress, who remarked upon the impropriety of such conduct in one who had been hopefully converted. Whereupon the sable empress retorted:

"I have 'sperienced religion, an' I'se gwine to jine the church, an be one ob de Lord's own lambs, but 'fore God, Miss B——, I'll scald that nigger furst!"

Why should female brokers alone be allowed in Wall street? Because Sing-Sing is the proper place for male-factors.

A Boston lecturer astonished his audience by bringing down his fist on the table and shouting. "Where is the religiosity of the anthropoid quadrumana?" If he thinks we have got it he can search us. We never saw it in the world.

A Vermont man has been arrested for killing his mother-in-law, supposing her to be a wild turkey. That's too thin. He knew she wasn't a turkey all the time. This outlandish way of putting a stop to mothers-in-law has got to be stopped, or the country will suffer.

The Rev. Mr. O—, a respectable clergyman, in the interior of the State, relates the following anecdote :

A couple came to him to be married. After the knot was tied, the bridegroom addressed him with—

"How much do you ax, mister ?"

"Why," replied the clergyman. "I generally take what is offered me. Sometimes more and sometimes less. I leave it to the bridegroom."

"Yes—but how much do you ax, I say ?" replied the happy man.

"I have just said," returned the clergyman, "that I left it to the decision of the bridegroom. Some give me ten dollars, some five, some three, some two, some one, and some only a quarter of a dollar."

"A quarter, eh ?" said the bridegroom; "well, that's as reasonable as a body could ax." He took out his pocket-book—there was no money there; he fumbled in all his pockets, but not a dime could he find. "I thought I had some money with me; but I recollect now, 'twas in my other trowsers-pocket. Hatty, have you got such a thing as a quarter about ye ?"

"Me," said the bride, with a mixture of shame and indignation. "I'm astonished at ye, to come here to be married without a cent to pay for it! If I'd knowed it afore, I wouldn't a come a step with ye; ye might have gone off alone to be married for all I care."

"Yes, but consider, Hatty," said the bridegroom, in a soothing tone, "we are married now, and it can't be helped—if you have got such a thing as a quarter of a dollar—"

"Here, take it," interrupted the angry bride, who, during the speech, had been searching in her work-bag; "and don't you," said she, with a significant motion of her finger—"don't you serve me another sich trick !"

Lord Fanshaw married his cook. On their bridal-day it rained tremendously; the coachman and his attendant sprites were wet through.

"Ah !" said a wag, "all quite in character—there's nothing but *dripping* wherever she goes."

A Cincinnatti girl sued a shoemaker because she couldn't get inside of a pair of shoes he made for her. He set up a plea that leather was scarce, and charged that she could have got them on easy enough if she had washed her feet. We don't usually publish " society items " in this column, but this is a subject that will interest all classes.

A Milwaukee woman, who had a child eaten by a hog, objected to having an officer kill the hog, as she had suffered bereavement enough for one mother. She promised to either keep the hog in a pen or keep the rest of her children in the house, so the hog was spared for family pork.

Notwithstanding the offers Chang and Eng have had to travel separate with rival shows, they have always stuck together, and have accumulated $200,000 worth of land and children. The story that they were not brothers, but cousins, is a base fabrication.

A Chicago mother left a six-months old baby in a crib, with a nursing bottle in its mouth, while she went to the court-house to see when that divorce suit was coming on. When she returned the child was dead, smothered with milk. She said she had often warned the baby to be careful about drinking too much.

"You flatter me," said a thin exquisite the other day to a young lady, who was praising the beauty of his moustache.

"For gracious sake, madam," interposed an old skipper, "don't make that monkey any flatter than he is now."

Judge B——, long a side judge under the " epaulet " system, when the real judge was flanked on each side by a man who was no lawyer, was asked if Judge Morrel ever consulted him in respect to any question.

"Yes," growled the old gentleman. "On the ninth day of Macdonald's trial for murder he asked me if my bones didn't ache."

Taking it Easy.

" Julius, what is the matter with the man ?"

"Sam, he's dead, he is."

"But haul him out of that pit."

" Yes, sir, but if you'd a hearn him holler ! It made me run."

" Why, how made you run?"

" Why, I thort as how it come from de bottom of de pit !"

" Here, you thick skull ! haul him out."

[*Meditative.*] " Too bad, too bad. Double work, first put him in, now pull him out. No, I'll let him *rusticate.*"

Flattering Preference.—Two natives of the Marquesas Islands have been carried to France. The story runs, that on the voyage one of their fellow-passengers, fishing for a compliment, asked them which they liked best, the French or English ? " The English," answered the man, smacking his lips, " they are the fattest." " And a great deal more tender," chimed in the woman, with a grin that exhibited two rows of pointed teeth as sharp as a crocodile's.

The Model Husband.—Mrs. Smith has company to dinner, and there are not strawberries enough, and as she looks at Mr. Smith with a sweet smile, and offers to help him, (at the same time kicking him gently with her slipper under the table,) he always replies, " No, I thank you, dear, they don't agree with me."

A Pennsylvania farmer had a warm time a few days since. He fainted away in his barn-yard, and his hogs took a lunch off of him, and he now carries both legs in a sling.

Some of these old editors who are near-sighted are trying to make the ladies believe that wearing low-necked dresses produces sore throat. It's all a confounded humbug, got up by the old buzzards who can't see.

A minister of a dry persuasion, at Lafayette, Ind. denounces the eating of oysters as a sin. That brother never could have said such a thing had he ever partaken of a Fulton-market fry of the saddle-rock gender. If eating these bivalve luxuries be a sin we stand ready to bet two to one that it was an oyster on the half shell that the "sarpint" tempted mother Eve with, instead of an apple. By-and-by these men of rectitude will pronounce it a sin to worry a lobster out of its shell, or to kiss your sweetheart.

The following crimes and offences may be committed without impunity and without fear of consequences:

Killing—time.
Murdering—in air.
Smothering—the feelings.
Stifling—a laugh.
Striking—a balance.
Forging—anchors.
Picking—your way.
Stealing—a kiss.
Coining—money.
Poaching—eggs.
Breaking into—a gallop.
Trespassing—on the attention.
Beating—carpets.
Cutting—jokes, and
Shooting—Niagara.

A colored member of the Georgia Legislature was killed by the door-keeper, and the Legislature decided to pay his salary to his widow, when six emphatic brunettes claimed the money. How these people do imitate white legislators.

A man in Buffalo pulled off his coat and jumped into the canal to save a woman from drowning, when a pickpocket stole his pocket-book from the coat, and the woman swore at him for pulling her hair in his efforts to save her life. Buffalo isn't much of a place to encourage heroism and self-sacrifice.

Mathematics.

"Sam, I suppose dat you've bin to school and read all froo your 'rithmatic?"

"Yes, sir, I've studied that branch of education."

"Well, now, suppose dat a turkey weighed twelve pounds six ounces and he cost a quarter ob a dollar compound. How many apple pie pans will it take fur to shingle a school-house?"

"I cannot really answer your problem."

"I can tell you."

"How many pans will you require?"

"Listen now. Ighsombromken wid de icks mock-combrusken und der alicotrusic mit das brumstic id de hocks mocks com trusic mid der Switzer kease. Don't you see?"

Love. :

"Sam, was you eber in lub?"

"No, Julius ; *you* have been, I understand."

"Yes, sir."

"How did you feel?"

"Why, I felt jist as if I was a big tunnel, and a train ob cars was comin in at both ends."

Wanted to Patent.—The *filter* of misfortune, to seperate true friends from de scum.

A Waterbury (Conn.) youth, repentant but incoherent over his dissipation, signed the following pledge : I solemnly promise to abstain from the use of all intoxicating beverages, otherwise than as a drink, and profanity, unless prescribed by a physician, at least four times a day, excepting cider."

There is a young lady in Glasgow who plays the concertina so well as to make ignorant people believe that it is a musical instrument.

Nothing to Take.—Hood was the parent of that unconscious remark of the child of a drunkard, who was said to take after his father. "Ah, father leaves nothing afterward to take."

Good Gramarian.

" Did you ever go to school, sir?"

" Oh yes, Massa."

" Then I suppose you studied Grammar?"

" Yes, sir, I did, and I'm some on Grammar, I am."

" Then I'll ask you a question."

" Go it."

" Parse the word ' Butter.'"

" Dat's kind ob slickery, but I can do it."

" Proceed, then."

" Butter am a common substantif, male gender, and agrees wid buckwheat cakes, is governed by sugar, molasses bein' understood."

The Weather no Joke.—An excited Editor's Opinion of a Hot Day.—" Yesterday was hot. Fat women felt fussy, and fanned furiously. Lean women leaned languidly on lounges, or lolled lazily like lilies on a lake. Shabby, slipshod sisters sat silently and sadly sweating in the shade, while soiled and sozzling shirt-collars and sticky shirts, stuck to such sap-heads as stirred in the sun. Babies bawled busily, and bit bobbins and bodkins till bed time. Literary gentlemen who undertook a heavy task of alliteration became exhausted in the middle of a weather paragraph, and gave it up for a cooler day. Yesterday was hot."

The Deluge.—A Scotchman and an Englishman were once disputing about the ancient origin of their respective families. The Englishman, getting out of patience, exclaimed, " Pooh! my friend, you'll tell me next that your ancestors were in the ark with Noah." " I've no preceece evedence o' the fac," replied the Scotchman; " but I've a shrewd conjecture that they were." " Very well," replied the Englishman, " all that may be possible, but to show you the immense superiority of my family at that time, I would inform you that they had a boat of their own."

What's What.

"Julius, what is de difference between dyin' an dieting?"

"Why, when you diet you expect it to take de color, and when you die you—do the same ting."

"No, Julius, I don't mean dat."

"What you mean den?"

"I mean die to be dead, and diet to abstain from high libbin'."

"Oh, ho! Dat's it, is it? Why, when you lib you don't die, an when you lib too high you are in danger ob dyin de oder way."

"Still you don't understand me. I mean to die, to gib up de ghost."

"Whose ghost? Oh! stop a-hittin me on de shins, you black nigger. Golly! I feel like dyin'."

"Then what is de difference?"

"I habn't dieted yet, and don't intend to, so I can't tell. Go 'way."

In a parlimentary committee for a new railway, it was necessary to prove populousness in a certain valley. The following questions and answers passed in the process.

"Do you mean to tell the committee," said counsel for the opponents of the new line, "that you ever saw an inhabited house in that valley?"

"Yes, I do," replied the witness.

"Did you ever see a vehicle there in all your life?"

"Yes, I did."

Some other questions were put, which led to nothing particular; but just as the witness was leaving the box, the learned gentleman put one more question.

"I am instructed to ask you if the vehicle you saw was not the hearse of the last inhabitant?"

"It was."

"What flower of beauty shall I marry?" asked a young spendthrift of his miserly governor. To which the governor replied, with a smile, "Marigold."

Western Serenade.

Clown.—Massa, I've trabeld ober de great West.
Master.—Then you've been West. In what state?
C.—Arkansaw, where ebery house is a log cabin; and I stopped at a tavern, and about one o'clock in de mornin, I heard a feller serenadin' his gal.
M.—What did he sing?
C.—This:

> Oh, Susey Rice,
> I've called you twice.
> I want you to wake,
> And see your Jake,
> And ope to me de door—
> Or winder—I don't care which—for
> It makes but little difference
> To eider you or I—
> Big pig, little pig,
> Root hog, or die.

And I tell you, massa, he got a mighty warm reception.
M.—He did?
C.—Yes, sir, a whole pail ob hot water.

The late Rev. Dr. Bethune once entered the crowded cabin of a Brooklyn ferry-boat, and while looking about for a seat suddenly heard himself addressed by name. Turning round he found a man standing, who said: "Doctor, take my seat; it's an honor to give such a man a seat. Ever since I heard of that big church in New York trying to get you away by giving a call of five thousand dollars, and you said you'd see 'em d—d first, I have had a great respect for you, and I think it an honor to give you a seat."

Shakspeare.

"Avaunt and quit my sight! Thy bones are marrowless—thy blood is cold—thou hast no speculation in those eyes, with which thou dost glare upon me,"—and thy head puts me in mind of—

"What, sir?"

"A worn-out mop."

The Man In The Moon.

"I heard 'em say dere was a man in de moon?"

" Yes. I believe it too."

" Why, dat's foolish."

" No, sir, for my wife sed she didn't know an oder man, nor want to, but me, and den she sed de *honey moon* was risin'."

The Soul.

"Sam, did you ever hear dat great preacher discourse about de soul?"

" No. What did he say."

" He sed de soul is a prisoner dat always kills its jailer when it makes its escape."

"Wery beautiful! But who did he say was the jailer?"

" He didn't say, but I s'pose it is de thread dat de shoe is sewed wid."

" Pompey, when I see you in de gutter I tink ob de philosopher who sed: "No man is so deep but has a shallow place."

" Jenny," said a landlady to her maid the other morning, " Jenny, was there any fire in the kitchen last night when you were sitting up?"

" Yes, marm," said Jenny, " there was a spark there when I went down, and I soon fanned it into flame."

The landlady looked suspiciously at Jenny, but she, innocent girl, went on scrubbing, and humming "Joe, the Postman."

An impecunious printer at Houston, Texas, wanted a printing press, and not having the wherewithal to purchase it, wrote to a man in New York, stating that if a press was not sent them immediately to print ballots with, the state would be "lost" to the Democrats. The press was sent, and Tracy, the sharper, rejoices in its possession. He is the champion confidence man of the Lone Star State.

Doctors.

"Mas—, can you tell me de fust ting a doctor does when he goes to see a sick man ?"

" Why, he looks at his tongue, of course."

" And can a doctor tell what's de matter wid de man by looking at his tongue ?"

" Of course."

" Den I want a doctor."

" Are you unwell, sir."

" No, but I've got a wagon dat's got somfin de matter wid it, and de wagon's got a tongue."

"May I sing, ma ?" asked a young lady of four who had been taken to church by her mother, and whose bump of music was doubtless excited by the performance to which she was listening. Ma, whose eye was upon the *paniers* in the next pew, of course said " Yes," as all indulgent mothers do ; and little hopeful with a strong voice, commenced " Up in a balloon." " Hush ! hush !" said ma, " don't sing that !" Pausing a moment, the young vocalist struck up " Not for Joe," and was immediately hustled out of the sanctuary.

How is this for High.—A boy was once watching some of his schoolfellows as they pelted an old gentleman's windows with snowballs. The old gentleman finally rushed out of the house, determined, if possible, to inflict some severe punishment on the offender, saying, when he caught the boy : "Now, you rascal, I'll whip you within an inch of your life !" Accordingly, he began to thrash him, when the boy immediately commenced laughing, and continued until the old gentleman desisted with the exclamation— "What are you laughing at ?" " Well, said the boy, " I'm laughing because you are awfully sold ; *I ain't the boy !*"

" My dear," said an affectionate spouse to her husband, " am I not your only treasure ?"

" Oh, yes," was the cool reply, " and I would willingly lay it up in heaven."

Stopped Sudden.

" Julius, I heard that an accident happened you lately ?"

" Yes, Sam, I fell off a ladder sixty-foot high."

" Did you hurt you much when you fell ?"

" Oh no, Sam, de fall didn't hurt me, it was stoppin' so sudden."

" How did the accident occur ?"

" After I got almost to de top ob de ladder a pig come and rubbed himself against de bottom and upset it."

That was a funny remark of the little girl who was sent out to hunt hen's eggs. She thought as she didn't find any, it was strange, as she saw " lots of hens standing around doing nothing."

A shoddy young lady surprised her mother on return-ing from a dance by saying that she enjoyed the " hugg-ing, set to music, most bullyly." She had reference to waltzing, and why isn't that a good name for it ? We think it a capital one.

" Have I not a right to be saucy, if I please ?" asked a young lady of an old bachelor.

" Yes, if you *please*, but not if you *dis*please.

Admitted.—Of all the strikes that inflict the greatest injury on the people, and leave nothing but bad blood and ill-feeling behind them, the policeman's strike is admitted to be the worst.

Happiness.—Among the " Wants " in one of our daily papers we see " Partial board for a single gentle-man ; house kept by a widow and daughter ; *busses* and cars convenient." Oh ! that we were a boarder !

At a sabbath-school at Burlington, Iowa, a pupil said that children were Christ's lambs. " Then, if the children are lambs, what are the old folks," asked a lady teacher. " Old bucks," answered a boy of the period.

Barber.

" Well, do you make plenty of money now, Julius ?''

" Pretty good deal ; but I am in de shavin' business."

"Indeed ! Well, how do you succeed as a fashion. able barber ?"

" Why, you see, Pompey, I charge six cents, an has a good many customers in de shavin line ; but when de liquor law goes in operation, I shall charge ten cents for a shave, and that is after the fourth of July."

" Why, Julius, what is the reason you intend to raise the price of shaving from six to ten cents after the fourth of July ?"

" Well, I make a close calculation, it will take so much more lather, because, you see, the faces of nine-tenths of my customers will then be one-third longer."

As the ferry boat was leaving the foot of Chambers street, N. Y., on Saturday, " Pat," the porter of the Spaulding House, Binghampton, had to make a jump of about three feet to get aboard. He was excited at the prospect of getting left, and jumped further than was necessary, landing among the chains, and rolling over against the ladies' cabin. Picking himself up, he looked at the gap between the boat and the shore, increased to about forty feet by the moving boat, scratched his head and said : " Howly Jabers, what a lep !" He thought he had made the biggest jump on record.

A Cool Philosopher.—A young chap boarded at one of the hotels in San Francisco, and managed for a long time, by one artifice or another, to postpone the payment of his bill. At last, the landlord became quite impatient, and stepping up to his boarder, slapped him gently on the shoulder, and asked him for some money. " I have not a red cent about me at present," was the laconic reply. " But, my dear sir," said the landlord, " I cannot afford to keep a boarding-house without being paid." " Well, sir," exclaimed our young philosopher, " if you cannot afford it, sell out to somebody who can"

Kisses.

" Julius, what is a kiss ?"

" A kiss is a buss."

" Suppose that you kiss a person's hand, what do you call it ?"

" A silly-buss."

" Now, then, if you should kiss everybody in the room, without regard to sex, what would you call that ?"

" An omni-buss."

" Suppose you kiss the wrong person ?"

" Why, dat would be a blunder-buss."

" Suppose you should go down in de kitchen and kiss the cook ?"

" Why, den you're gone, sure."

"How is that ?"

" 'Case you'll bus-t your biler."

A lively demand for tracts at a Western settlement recently encouraged the hopes of the Tract Society that an immense work of revival must be going on there. The cry was constantly for "tracts, more tracts." At last it leaked out that the settlers were using these promoters of faith, not for moral comfort, but to paper their log cabins with. The Tract Society since the discovery, is a wiser, but sadder institution.

A disappointed young man, whose girl had "gone back " on him, went to a Muscatine drug store the other night, and called for a dose of cold poison. The druggist surmised his purpose, and, without saying anything, gave him, instead of poison, a powerful emetic. It had a good effect, as he soon threw up his sad spirits, and begged lustily for his life.

A committee appointed to investigate an alleged charge of undue punishment inflicted by a school teacher reported "that the punishment was not actuated by malice, but was occasioned by an undue appreciation of the thickness of the boy's pantaloons."

Paddy's "Excelsior."

'Twas growing dark so terrible fasht,
Whin through a town up the mountain there pashed
A broth of a boy to his neck in the shnow,
As he walked, his shillalah he swung to and fro,
Saying, it's up to the top I'm bound for to go,
  Be jabers !

He looked mortal sad, and his eyes were as bright,
As a fire of turf on a cowld winter night,
And a divil a word that he said could ye tell,
As he opened his mouth and let out a yell,
It's up to the top of the mountain I'll go,
Onless covered up with this bothersome shnow,
  Be jabers !

Through the windows he saw as he traveled along,
The light of the candles and fires so warm,
But a big chunk of ice hung over his head,
Wid a shiver and groan, by St. Patrick ! he said,
It's up to the very tip-top I will rush,
And then if it falls it's not meself it'll crush,
  Be jabers !

Whist a bit ! said an owld man, whose head was as white
As the shnow that fell down on that miserable night ;
Shure, ye'll fall in the wather, me bit of a lad,
For the night is so dark and the walkin' so bad,
Bedad ! he'd not lisht to a word that was said,
But he'd go to the top if he went on his head,
  Be jabers !

A bright buxom young girl, such as like to be kissed,
Axed him wudn't he sthop, and how could he resist ?
So, snapping his fingers, and winking his eye,
While shmiling upon her, he made this reply—
Faith, 1 meant to kape on till I got to the top,
But as your shwate self has axed me, 1 may as well shtop,
  Be jabers !

He shtopped all night and he shtopped all day,
And ye mustn't be axin when he did go away;
Fur wudn't he be a bastely gossoon
To be lavin' his darlint in the shwate honey-moon?
Whin the old man has praties enough and to spare,
Shure he might as well shtay, if he's comfortable there,
     Be jabers!

Book-Keeper.

"Sam, why don't you come down to the store and see me?"

"To the store! What do you do in a store?"

"Why, Sam, I am a clerk."

"Oh, yes. Well, what do you have to do?"

"Not much. I go down in the morning about five o'clock, sweep out the store, make de fires, take down de shutters, wait on de ladies, &c. Oh, Sam! I don't hab much to do."

"I suppose your employer places great confidence in you?"

"Yes; the boss went out of town the other day, an left me in charge of de bisness. We done a first-rate bisness that day, an when the boss came back, he went behind the counter, opened the drawer to see how much money had been taken, an he found that it *had all been taken*."

"Then, I suppose, you were taken?"

"Yes; the proprietor had me down to the police court, an a man that was in the store swore that he see me take the money, an they was jest a goin to send me up to whar dey sing twice, but I told the judge it was not right to commit me, for there was but one man swore that he see me take the money, an I could go out and get two hundred that would swear they *didn't* see me take it; so they let me go."

"What are you doing now?"

"I got another place. I am a book-keeper now."

"How do you keep books?"

"Easy enough. I takes 'em home at night, keeps 'em till next day, an' den brings 'em back again."

"Is it a goo— situation ?"

"First-rate. I get seven dollars a month."

"Surely, that's very good."

"Yes, sir ; seven dollars a month an' found."

"That's better still."

"And I get one month's wages in advance."

"When do you go to work?"

"Just as soon as the man finds me."

"What will you do then ?"

"Why, I'll get another month's wages an' let him find me again."

A woman in Indiana prays that she may be cut loose from her husband, giving as a reason that he has only bought her a pair of shoe-strings since their marriage. We sympathize with the woman. Such a wardrobe as that must be rather cool at this season of the year, to say nothing of how a woman must look dressed only in a pair of shoe-strings.

One Sunday morning as a flock of the faithful were wending their way to the village church they were surprised to find the building closed, the bell silent, and no evidence that a congregation were expected to assemble. The astonishment of the brethren and sisters was somewhat relieved by the sudden discovery of the following placard :

"This 'ere plais is klozed for repairs onto the preacher. His voice is gin eout, & we've sent him to Saratogy to recooper it, onto ful-pay. Sinners under konvickshun is respeckfully requested to adjurn to Saratogy, eff they have the stamps. Eff not, to hold til the Fall term. Eff they konclude to die in the meantime, your preacher will maik it awl rite with 'em in the nex wurld."

Slender party (who is not very comfortable)—"These street cars ought to charge by weight." Stout party (sharply)—"Ah ! if they did they would never stop to pick you up."

Lap Dog.

"Sam, I heard somefin' 'bout Pompey yesterday."

"What is it, Julius!"

"Why, he went down to see his gal night afore last, an' his gal has got a pooty little dog an' she was hug-gin' an' kissin' de dog, when Pompey got jealous."

"What did he say?"

"Sez he to de gal, 'Jane, why don't you kiss me like you do de little dog?'"

"What answer did she make?"

"Why, she tole him dat she didn't kiss ebery puppy dat come along."

"Sam, what's next to de oyster?"

"I really don't know, Julius."

"Why, de shell, ob course."

A greenhorn sat a long time, very attentive, musing upon a cane-bottom chair. At length he said:

"I wonder what fellow took the trouble to find all them ar holes, and put straws around 'em."

A Boston undertaker having established himself next door to a popular livery stable, was accosted one day by an individual, apparently in a great hurry, who asked, "Can I get an open buggy here?" "No sir," said the interrogated, "we haven't got a buggy, but, (pointing to a hearse which stood at the door) we can accommodate you with a *skeleton wagon!*"

General Wood says, in writing from Brazil, that the ladies, on being introduced to a stranger, insist upon being embraced, "heart throbbing against heart." Ho, for Brazil!

A Hotel at Red Oak, Iowa, advertises: "The most polite ladies will act as waiters, dresssd in pea-green jackets, tilting hoops, and high-heeled buttoned gaiters." How about the hash? That's of more importance to a hungry man than pea-green jackets or buttoned-up hoops.

Lola Montez.

"Jake, did you eber hear Lola Montez lecture?"

"Bless your heart, no."

"Wall, I did."

"What did she say?"

"I can't recollect, but—she sed de man always lubs de woman and de woman does what she wants wid him."

"No sir-ee, dat aint right."

"Well, she said Ebe tempted Adam, and crammed an apple in his troat, and so it has been eber since, an I know what she sez is all right, for de newspapers all say de same ting."

"Oh, Adam wasn't no man, den."

"Wasn't no man?"

"No, he was defunct afore dat occurred."

"Was what?"

"He was *dead* in lub wid Ebe."

Alas! that there should be so many poor souls who, in this world, and that which is to come, look forward to nothing that is substantially comfortable and satisfying! Here, for instance, is a veritable descendant of St. Martha, who came into a neighbor's house a few days since, downcast, wearying with many cares and cumbered with much serving, "So much to do! cleaning, working, cooking, washing, sewing, and everything else! No rest! never was, never will be for me!"

"O, yes," said the good woman she addressed, "there will be a rest one day for us all—a long rest."

"Not for me! not for me," was the reply. "Whenever I *do* die, there will be certain to be resurrection *the very next day!* It would be just my luck!'

Tit-for-Tat.—George Coleman getting out of a hackney coach one night, gave the driver a shilling. "This is a bad shilling, sir," said the driver. "Then it is all right," said George, with his inimitable chuckle, "it is all right—yours is a bad coach."

Why are a young lady's affections always doubtful? Because they are miss-givings.

Bank Note.

" Julius, what was that man tryin' to sell you yesterday ?"

" It was a bank-note detector."

" Did you buy one ?"

" No."

" Why not ?"

" I tole de man dat I would buy one if he could detect a bank-note in my pocket."

False Witness.—The children at a Sunday-school not long since, being asked, among other questions, what bearing false witness against one's neighbor meant, a pert little girl replied : " That it was when nobody hain't done nothing, and somebody goes and tells."

Jones thinks that soda-water is not reliable for a steady drink. It is too gassy. The next morning after drinking thirty-eight bottles he found himself full of gas and as tight as a balloon. He hadn't an article of clothing that he could wear except his umbrella.

Chilicothe, Ohio, is having fun with one of those careful ministers. His name is Charles F. Blank. He has been acting so with the wife of the sexton of the church that they couldn't take any comfort with him. All of which comes from not sowing one's " wild oats" before one gets into the " cloth."

Young lady (to Fred, with thin legs)—" Fred, I always admired your courage. I knew when I first laid my eyes on you, that you were brave to rashness." Fred (coming up smiling)—" Oh ! don't my dear ? Why do you say that ?" Young lady—" Why any man must have courage who can trust himself long at a time on such legs as yours."

At Cedar Falls, Iowa, they get mad if a man goes into the theater with a cigar in his mouth and puts his heels on the shoulders of the man in front of him. A man got arrested just for that out there. There is no sociability about some people.

Perpetuating Life.

"Julius, I hab found out a new way ob perpetuating my life."

"Pompey, is that so? If it is original it must be good."

"Yes, Julius. I claimed it as original though others had employed it before me."

"Then it can't be original."

"Yes, sir, it is."

"Well, let's hab it, Pompey?"

"*Stump* de State for political candidates, an' you will get a *strong* name; den go and rob a bank an dat builds your fame, for Ole Massa Antony sed when he buried de great fader ob your name, Julius, "de evil dat men do will live after dem."

"Den de argument is, dat stump speaking is evil?"

"Yes, ob course, if you look at it as I look, an' many oders do, to carry out dere *base* purpose."

"Oh, I see. It is de *foundation* ob evil."

"Yes, and de root ob all (subsequent) evil."

At Terre Haute, Ind., a man "reproved" his wife with an ax handle, breaking a lot of her ribs. He should be "reasoned" with a piece of rope.

On the arrival of an emigrant ship, some years ago, when the North Carolina lay off the Battery, an Irishman, hearing the guns fired at sunset, inquired of one of the sailors what it was.

"What's that? Why, that's sunset," was the contemptous reply.

"Sunset!" Paddy exclaimed, with distended eyes, "sunset? Howly Moses! and does the sun always go down in this country with such a whack as that?"

Why is a newspaper reporter like a pickpocket?

Because he takes notes and must have nimble fingers to ensure success.

Why, if my father has ten sisters may it be inferred that I have leased property?

Because I have ten aunts (*tenants*).

A Californian proposes a pretty little job to Congress. He owns, he writes, a number of silver mines: "I own millions and millions of feet of affluent silver leads in Nevada—in fact, I own the entire undercrust of that country, nearly; and if Congress would move that State off my property so that I could get at it, I would be wealthy yet."

A person at Liverpool, England, writes to Milwaukee to get information as to the whereabouts of one John Smith, but the papers there are unable to find him. We don't want to press our services upon the man, but there *was* a John Smith in one of the Wisconsin regiments during the war. It might be well to write to him.

The Spaniards are not commonly supposed to be a progressive people, and yet it is certain that at this moment Spain is the most rising country in Europe, not excepting even Ireland.

A Boston lady going through Kansas, saw an animal near the depot, and asked a boy if it was a buffalo. Her curiosity was satisfied when he replied. "No ma'am. Them's a muil!" Restoratives were immediately applied, and she enjoyed a good night's rest.

A noted Western Express Company prints on its shipping receipts that it will not be liable for "any loss or damage by fire, the acts of God or Indians, or other enemies of the government."

A girl in Chester, Vt., has died from tight lacing. These corsets should be done away with, and if the girls can't live without being squeezed we suppose men can be found who would sacrifice themselves. As old as we are, we had rather devote three hours a day, without a cent of pay, as a brevet corset, than see these girls dying off in that manner. Office hours almost any time.

Stays.

" Bosh, did you eber see a pair of stays?"

" Take care an' don't insult me."

" How is dat goin' to insult you I should like to know?"

" Why, I wore 'em."

" You wore 'em?   Ha! ha!"

" Yes, wen I in de State's prison."

" Oh, I don't mean dat kind ob stays : I mean ladies corsets."

" No, Sam, I neber seed any ob dem, but I'se seen Uncle Sam's stays."

" Bosh, dat was witty."

" Yes, sir.   I always *wet-tea* afore I hans it round."

"Sam, de most curious ting I eber see was dat a watch always keeps so dry."

" Why, Julius?"

" 'Case dars a running spring inside ob it."

Why are persons with short memories like office holders?

Because they are always for getting everything.

THE END.

Popular Books.—Sent post-paid at the Prices Marked

Wehman's Parlor Conjurer. A capital little hand-book of parlor magic, sleight of hand, card tricks, coin tricks, and directions for the construction and use of conjurer's implements. Sent by mail, post-paid, on receipt of **10 Cents.**

Wehman's Black Art; or Magic Made Easy. A full and complete description and explanation of all kinds of sleight-of-hand tricks and conjuring with cards and coins, as performed by the most renowned prestidigitators and conjurors; together with wonderful experiments in magnetism, chemistry, electricity, and fireworks, so simplified as to be adapted for amusement in the home circle. Sent by mail, post-paid, on receipt of **10 Cents.**

Mother Shipton's Gipsy Fortune-Teller and Dream BOOK. With NAPOLEON'S ORACULUM. Embracing full and correct rules of divination concerning dreams and visions, foretelling of future events, their scientific application to Physiognomy, Physiology, Moles, Cards, Dice, Dominoes, Grounds of Coffee and Tea Cups, etc., together with the application and observance of Charms, Spells and Incantations, It also gives the true interpretations of dreams, and the lucky numbers of the lottery to which they apply. Sent by mail, post-paid, on receipt of **10 Cents.** U. S. postage stamps taken same as cash.

Albertus Magnus; or Egyptian Secrets. Being the approved, verified, sympathetic and natural Egyptian secrets, or white and black art for man and beast. The book of nature and hidden secrets and mysteries of life unveiled; being the forbidden knowledge of ancient philosophers, by that celebrated student, philosopher, chemist, etc., etc. This extraordinary work, sometimes called the great "Pow How; or, Magic Cure Book," is held by thousands to be the only sure means to avoid sickness in their families; to make them fortunate in their crops and stock raising, and prosperous in all their undertakings. enabling them to acquire wealth, honor and esteem amongst their friends and neighbors. Price **ONE DOLLAR** per copy. or **3 copies**, to one address, for **$2.00.** U. S. postage stamps taken same as cash.

The Sixth and Seventh Books of Moses. Translated under our personal supervision into the English language, and published by us for the first time. With exact copies of over 125 seals, signs, emblems, etc., used by Moses, Aaron, Israelites, Egyptians, etc., in their astonishing magical and other arts, including the period of time covered by the Old and New Testament. This wonderful translation is of great importance to the Christian, Deist, Jew or Gentile, Episcopalian or Roman Catholic, and dissenters of every denomination. The extracts from the old and rare Mosaic books of the Talmud and Cabala are invaluable. It is from the German translation that we have produced the English edition of the Sixth and Seventh Books of Moses. The German work has for some time largely circulated in Germany and among the Germans of this country, and is pronounced the most wonderful work ever published. So true is this that many millions of Germans and others of German education never undertake any important step in life relating to finance, exchange, or health without seeking from its pages advice and guidance. The magic of the Israelites is fully explained— such as second sight, healing the sick, spiritual and sensual affection, divine inspiration, mesmeric clairvoyance, etc. The engravings of signs in this work are exact copies of the Israelites' and Egyptians' to accomplish the designs for good or evil, and are separately explained. This book has become enormously popular. Beware of humbugs. Vols. 1 and 2 bound together in one volume. Price reduced to **$1.00** per copy, or **3 copies for $2.00.** U. S. postage stamps taken same as cash

---

ADDRESS ALL ORDERS TO

HENRY J. WEHMAN, Publisher, 108 Park Row, New York

Popular Books.—Sent post-paid at the Prices Marked

De Witt's Superior School Dialogues. As the title suggests, so the contents of this book. Containing carefully selected pieces for school, academy and exhibition use. Its salient features are quality, quantity, and small price. Sent by mail, post-paid, on receipt of **10 Cents.** U. S. postage stamps taken same as cash.

De Witt's Thespian School Dialogues. Containing a choice selection of dialogues suitable for private theatricals, and for the use of dramatic associations. These pieces are all eminently dramatic, affording every young person a chance to show his particular genius. Sent by mail, post-paid, on receipt of **10 Cents.**

Webster's Progressive Speaker. A very fine selection of most admirable pieces. Just the thing needed in the higher classes of schools, and for pleasant home entertainments. Well printed, from clear, readable type, and bound in handsome colored cover. Sent by mail, post-paid, on receipt of **25 Cents.** U. S. postage stamps taken same as cash.

De Witt's Perfection School Dialogues. By O. Augusta Cheney. Containing the following dialogues, viz:—The Ghostly Visitation—Practical Husbandry—Mr. Smith's Day at Home—The Country Cousin—Taking Position—Deacon Robison's Present—Mrs. Marc' Lesson—The Magic Mirror. Sent by mail, post-paid, on receipt of U. S. postage stamps taken same as cash.

Webster's Youthful Speaker. Containing a great nu ber of choice, eloquent, and effective pieces, eminently suitable for d lamation by intermediate pupils in school exhibitions, and on simil occasions. Well printed on good paper, from clear, readable type, an bound in handsome colored cover. Sent by mail, post-paid, on receipt o **Twenty-five Cents.** U. S. postage stamps taken same as cash.

De Witt's Academic School Dialogues. By O. Augusta Cheney. Containing the following selection of popular dialogues, viz.:—Mr. Bliss' Vision—High Life Below Stairs—Boarding on a Farm—Taming a Wife—John Smith's Trials—Aunt Rachel's Fright—The Hypochondriac Cured—Aunt Patience's Ear-Trumpet. Sent by mail, post-paid, on receipt of **10 Cents.** U. S. postage stamps taken same as cash.

De Witt's Platform School Dialogues. By Horatio Alger and O. Augusta Cheney. A carefully selected collection of dialogues that have nearly all been used at exhibitions in different parts of the country, and met with great success, which led to their publication. Although meant for representation, readers will find them a source of entertainment. These pieces are the best of their kind. Sent by mail, post-paid, on receipt of **10 Cents.** U. S. postage stamps taken same as cash.

Wehman's Recitations for Christmas. Edited by Margaret Holmes. Sixty choice selections from the best writers, suitable for use in Christmas entertainments in church and school. Among the authors represented are Dickens, Aldrich, Howells, Lew Wallace, R. H. Stoddard, John Boyle O'Reilly, Herrick, Coleridge, Geo. W. Curtis, Margaret Holmes. Thomas Nelson Page, Julia Goddard, Phœbe Cary, and Thomas Hood. Well printed, from clear, readable type, and bound in handsome colored cover. Sent by mail, post-paid, on receipt of **25 cts.**

ADDRESS ALL ORDERS TO

HENRY J. WEHMAN, Publisher, 108 Park Row, New York

Popular Books.—Sent post-paid at the Prices Marked

Wehman's Book on Base-Ball. Full directions for playing the American national game. The revised rules of the game, with explanatory notes, instructions for scoring, etc. Sent by mail, post-paid, on receipt of **10 Cents.**

Wehman's Rowing and Sculling. Full instructions as to the selection and use of all manner of rowboats, from the eight-oared barge to the single scull. Also, a chapter on canoeing. Sent by mail, post-paid, on receipt of **10 Cents.**

Wehman's Cricket and La Crosse. Plain, full and accurate information and instruction for playing the English national game of cricket, and the Canadian game of la crosse, with the revised rules. Sent by mail, post-paid, on receipt of **10 Cents.**

Wehman's Boxing and Wrestling. Gives full directions in regard to the various positions, modes of attack and defence, training, etc. With numerous illustrations. Sent by mail, post-paid, on receipt of **10 Cents.** U. S. postage stamps taken same as cash.

Wehman's Draughts, Backgammon, Dominoes AND SOLITAIRE. Rules for beginners in these well-known and popular household games, with a large number of interesting and instructive problems. Sent by mail, post-paid, on receipt of **10 Cents.**

Owen Swift's Boxing Without a Master. Explained in so easy a manner that any person may comprehend this useful art. Containing descriptions of correct pugilistic attitudes, feints, blows and guards, as practised by the most celebrated boxers of the past and present. With numerous spirited engravings. By Owen Swift, Master of the art of boxing. Sent by mail, post-paid, on receipt of **15 Cents.**

De Witt's American Chess Manual. By an old player. Containing full instructions for players. Also, the new rules of the game as adopted by the American Chess Association. Together with an account of the American Chess Congresses held since 1857, and the records of Chess Tourneys, with a choice selection of end games, problems, etc. Edited by Henry Chadwick. Sent by mail, post-paid, on receipt of **10 Cents.** U. S. postage stamps taken same as cash.

Wehman's Art of Swimming. A plain and practical treatise (illustrated) upon this most useful and invigorating pastime, teaching how to swim backwards, forwards and sideways, on or under the water, and to dive, leap and float in every possible manner. To which is appended the most approved and certain method of saving life from drowning and resuscitating the apparently lifeless. By Charles Weightman, the Man Fish. Sent by mail, post-paid, on receipt of **25 Cents.**

Wehman's Book on the Art and Science of Boxing AND SELF-DEFENCE. A full knowledge of the rules laid down in this book, and a careful study of the plates thereto attached will enable one to "hold his own" wheresoever he may go and with whomsoever he may come in contact. The pictures show every possible attitude for blow, feint, stop, dodge or get-away. A voluminous outline of the lives of a large number who have entered the ring to prove their prowess is appended as examples of what may be achieved by thorough training. It also contains the "London Prize Ring Rules" and "Revised Queensbury Rules." Sent by mail, post-paid, on receipt of **25 Cents.**